How The Puppy Learned To Cherish Lif(

ISBN- 9780578608150

How The Puppy Learned To Cherish Life is written to encourage the young and old to cherish God's gift of life and to live nobly. The purpose of the copyright is to prevent the reproduction, misuse, and abuse of the material. Please address all requests for information or permission to:

Dr. Patrick Hunt
M2E Motivational Consulting
On the Web: www.higherplace.net

Dedication

This story is dedicated to my wife, children, and grandchildren.

Acknowledgements

Thanks to family and friends who encouraged me in the publication of this book. A special thank you is given to my wife, Terry, for their editorial assistance. Gratitude is expressed to Dr. Denny Bates for assistance in getting this book onto Amazon KDP. Pictures are from personal and Shutterstock photos.

Happy Times:

There was once a farmer named Joshua. He lived on a farm that was passed down to him from his parent. His family had owned this farm for over 200 years. The farm had a large river; it also had numerous lakes, mature forests, and very high hills. The farm also had many animals. Some of the animals were domesticated and some of the animals were wild. However, there was something very special about this farm and its animals - they could talk to each other. Joshua and his family were kind people; they enjoyed working and playing with all of the animals on their farm. They also enjoyed watching the animals work and play with each other.

On one spring day, Joshua's family and the animals were very happy; a new puppy and a new pony had been born. The puppy's name was Molly and the pony's name was Tony. They soon became very good friends. They loved to run across meadows and through the forest. Along the way, they would make some of the birds spring to flight. Molly and Tony would laugh, and the pheasants would also laugh. The pheasants would shout that Molly and Tony were not nearly as fast as them. What's more, they would prove it as they flew over Molly and Tony's heads and up to the top of the hills. As the two played, they often jumped into the lakes with big splashes. This always made the ducks and geese scatter. Even so, the ducks and geese would laugh and tell them: We can swim faster and fly faster than you! Molly and Tony's lives were filled with joy.

Unhappy Times:

Sadly, one day when Molly went to the barn to find Tony, she saw Mr. Joshua and two of his children. They were with the animal doctor. One of the older sheep, Ms. Mary, told Molly that Tony was very sick. He was so sick that he could not even stand up. Upon hearing this news, Molly quickly ran to find her mother. She asked her: Why is Tony sick? Then she quickly asked: Would he soon be well? Her mother told her that usually young ponies would get well quickly, but sometimes they were too sick. In those cases, the young ponies just like the old ponies would die. Molly was frightened by this news. She and her mother quickly ran back to the barn to check on Tony. When she arrived, her heart sank. She saw Mr. Joshua and his children with their heads down walking away with the doctor. As they stood there, Ms. Mary came up to Molly and said: We are all very sad because Tony has died. This news was more than Molly could bear.

She ran through the meadows, but she could not hear the laughing pheasants. She did not receive any joy when she ran by the squirrels as they exclaimed: come catch me. She was not able to receive any joy from the baby rabbits that played jump-over me games as she slowly walked up the hill. When she got near the top of the hill, she could see the big river and the waterfall that crashed onto the rocks below: She thought that she could never again have joy without her friend Tony.

In her brokenhearted condition, she began to talk out loud. She said: Maybe I should go to the big river, jump in, and die on the rocks below. Then she said: I think this would be better than living with the pain of my broken heart. Fortunately, she had stopped beneath one of the grand old trees. These trees had stood on the top of the hill for over 200 years. This particular grand tree was the home of a very wise old owl named Solomon. He had heard Molly speaking of her broken heart. Most importantly, he had heard her speaking of how she did not think she could go on living. He had also heard her speak of jumping in the big river and going over the waterfall. Mr. Solomon, in his wisdom, knew that this was very serious. So he said: Molly, I know that you have a very sad and broken heart. Broken hearts are terrible; they are very hard to bear. Many with such grief and sorrow have sat on this hill beneath these grand trees.

Over my life, I have seen and heard many stories about broken hearts. I also have heard stories from my parents and my grandparents. Like Mr. Joshua and his family, my family has lived here for more than 200 years. We have seen great sadness and great joy for Mr. Joshua and his family as well as all the animals of the farm. He paused and then he said: Molly, think how sad your mother would be if you are not here and if she could not see you running through the meadows. Think of how sad the pheasants, rabbits, and geese would be if they could not play games with you. Also, think about how sad Mr. Joshua and his family would be if they did not get to see you grow up to be a mama and have your little puppies to run through the meadows and swim in the lakes. Additionally, you will be alive and able to do noble things to help Mr. Joshua and the other animals. Then he paused again before he said: Molly, my dear little puppy your broken heart will be healed; you will again have happy days.

When Molly had heard the words of the wise old owl, Mr. Solomon, she decided he was right. Her pain would pass someday, and her broken heart could heal. As she walked back to the farmhouse not all the animals noticed her broken heart, but Mr. Joshua noticed her. He picked her up, rubbed her head, and stroked her back. He said: Molly, we will always remember Tony and the friendship that you had with him. We will also look forward to the days that you will again run through the meadows and swim in the lakes. Mr. Joshua also told her that he had just the right friend for her. His name was Mr. Clyde, the very large and elderly Clydesdale horse. Then he told Molly to go home to her parents because they were extremely worried. When Molly arrived home, her parents were overjoyed to see her. Furthermore, they knew Mr. Clyde: They thought he would be an excellent friend for Molly. So, the next day, Molly and Mr. Clyde went to the meadow.

Better Times:

Mr. Clyde was so large that he provided shade for Molly when she wanted to get out of the sun. Even better, when they went to the lake, he would make a path through the cattails and bulrush. The path was so large that it was easy for Molly to jump in and swim. In the lake, she could even ride on his back as he swam through the deep water. They also had great times watching the little lambs and goats play chase and jump-over me. Sometimes, Molly would join in with the chase games. At other times, the little goats and lambs would play chase around Mr. Clyde's huge legs. Two of the little lambs, Ruth and Boaz, were Molly's favorites; they were the great grandchildren of her friend, Ms. Mary. As time went by, Molly would tell Mr. Clyde about her friend, Tony, and Mr. Clyde would tell her about the great times he had pulling the wagons.

He would tell her about the many rides that Mr. Joshua took on the wagons when he was a boy. He also told her how Mr. Joshua played with Molly's great grandma when she was a puppy. As time went on, Molly's broken heart began to heal, and she started having fun doing the things that she loved. Her days again were filled with work and play on Mr. Joshua's farm.

Thankful Times:

Many years later, when Molly was an old dog she took a walk across the meadows and up the big hill. And there she sat under the grand old tree. Mr. Solomon was no longer there. In his place sat his son, Mr. Moses. He leaned over and said: Well good afternoon Ms. Molly; how are you today! She said, I am very well thank you. Then she said: Mr. Moses, do you know that I am now a great-great great -grandmother. He said: Now isn't that grand. I've seen your descendants running around the meadows and swimming in the lakes.
Then, Molly paused before she said: Neither my descendants nor I would be here today had it not been for your wise father, Mr. Solomon. He stopped me from jumping in the big river and going over the waterfall when my heart was broken.

Then, Mr. Moses said, Oh yes, Ms. Molly, my father taught me that we must always cherish life. He learned that truth from his parents. It has been passed down in our family on these trees and on this farm for over 200 years.
Then, Ms. Molly took a deep breath and said: Mr. Moses, let's watch the sun go down while we cherish both the remains of this day and life.

THE END

John 10:10 - *I have come that they may have life, and have it to the full.*

Dr. Patrick Hunt grew up in North Carolina where his mother's family had lived for over 200 years. In contrast, his father was second-generation Irish from New York. His father worked in the heating and air-conditioning industry. He was a purple-heart veteran of World War II. His mother was a schoolteacher and a homemaker. She loved to tell stories as well as write poems and essays. His family owned a farm which was only 2 miles from his grandparents' farm. The farms had animals, fields, and woodlands along with springs, streams, and ponds. It was there that he, his sister, and many relatives played and worked. It was from his family and their Presbyterian Church that his character, imagination, and dreams were formed. The community of his childhood was also the community of his wife. They have been soulmates on this journey of life for over 50 years.

Dr. Hunt started his education with a bachelor degree from Clemson University. He then received his PhD from the University of Florida. The faculties of both these prestigious universities greatly affected the professional skills and philosophies of Dr. Hunt. After receiving his PhD, he served a tour in the U.S. Army. At the time of his discharge, he was a captain. He holds in highest regard the men and women with whom he served.

He has a great love for research and development. He was blessed to work this first five years of his career at the huge research and development center of the U.S. Army Corps of Engineers –the Waterways Experiment Station. After this assignment, he transferred to the US Department of Agriculture's Agricultural Research Service. He became the Research Leader and Director of the Coastal Plains Soil, Water, and Plant Research Center. He held this position for 37 years. He retired after a distinguished forty-year career as an agricultural scientist. There he published more than 150 peer-reviewed scientific papers. He is a Fellow of four scientific societies.

Throughout his career his wife and family were always a priority. He and his wife were involved in their children's activities, dreams, and character development. They are similarly involved in the lives of their grandchildren.

Dr. Hunt is now involved in the exhortation and encouragement of both the young and old. He writes and speaks about the principles of productive and fulfilled lives. Additionally, he writes Christian books and tracts that are applicable to both teenagers and adults. He also writes children's stories that teach children to cherish life and live nobly. He is hopeful that the materials on his website (drpatrickhunt.com) along with his books will be both comforting and inspirational.